Little Panda

by Sherry Bowen
illustrated by Chad Wallace

Richard C. Owen Publishers, Inc.
Katonah, New York

Little Panda loved to eat
and eat and eat and eat.

Mama Panda said,
"Be careful what you eat, Little Panda.
You'll get a rumbly, grumbly tummy ache."

Little Panda ate crunchy leaves.
He ate pretty flowers.
He ate little twisty vines.

His mother mostly ate bamboo.

Soon Little Panda felt full and happy.

But then . . .

"Rumble, rumble," his tummy rumbled.
"Grumble, grumble," his tummy grumbled.

"Rumble, rumble! Grumble, grumble!"

"Mama! Mama!" cried Little Panda,
"I have a rumbly, grumbly tummy ache."

"Poor Little Panda," said Mama Panda.
"I love you. I am so sorry you have
a tummy ache. What did you eat?" she asked.

"I ate leaves and flowers
and little twisty vines.
They tasted so good!" said Little Panda.

“I am sure they did,” said Mama Panda,
“but please be careful what you eat.
You know . . .

little pandas should
mostly eat bamboo."